This book belongs to...

This book is dedicated to my beautiful Marlo May.

Why Don't You Love Me?

Written and Illustrated by Nicola L Meekin

There was once a little dog
called Marlo.

She was small, white and
very fluffy.

Marlo lived with her human Dad,

Mum and Brother.

Her Brother, Alfie, was a teenager.

He was always looking at a small object in his hand.

The object seemed to light up his face.

Also, most days, Alfie had some strange things over his ears.

They seemed to stop him from hearing a knock at the door, or Mum shouting "tea's ready!"

Most morning's Marlo would jump up and down, in front of Alfie.

She would wag her tail and offer her favourite toy, in the hope that her Brother would play.

But there was no reaction from
Alfie, as he was too busy,

staring at the object in his hand.

This made Marlo feel very sad.

"Why don't you love me?"

Thought the little dog.

At midday, Marlo loved to sit on the back of the sofa.

She would spend most of the afternoon looking out of the window, watching the world go by.

There was a striped cat, that would climb over the wall and would walk past the window, where the little dog sat.
Marlo wanted to say "Hello" to the cat. She would shout to tell her Mum.

But, all her Mum heard was
"Bark, Bark, Bark!"

So Mum would tell the little dog to
"stop barking!"
And to "be quiet!"

This made Marlo feel very sad.

"Why don't you love me?"

Thought the little dog.

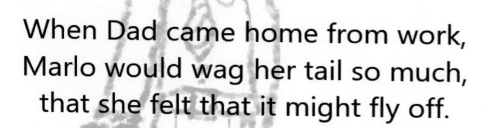

When Dad came home from work,
Marlo would wag her tail so much,
that she felt that it might fly off.

Dad would come in through the front door, walk straight past the little dog, and give Mum a kiss on the cheek.

This made Marlo feel very sad.

"Why don't you love me?"

Thought the little dog.

Every day at five 'o' clock,
Mum would shout "Marlo"
from the kitchen.

In the kitchen, there was always a bowl full of delicious food, for Marlo to eat.

She would lap up the food, enjoying every last bit.

This made Marlo
feel very happy.

"Mum really loves me!"
Thought the little dog.

At six 'o' clock, Alfie would shout "walkies!"

Alfie and Marlo would go for a walk to the field, at the end of the street. There they would play fetch, with the little dogs favourite toy.

When they arrived home, Alfie
would say "good girl!"

This made
Marlo feel very
happy.

"Alfie really loves me!"

Thought the little dog.

At seven 'o' clock, Dad would
usually be reading the
newspaper.

Marlo would climb up onto
Dads lap to get warm.

Dad would pat her on her
head, and stroke her back.

This made Marlo
feel very happy.

"Dad really loves me!"

Thought the little dog.

After a very busy day, the little dog was very tired.

Every night when the stars came out, and everyone was in bed.

The little dog fell asleep, knowing that she was loved.

And still to this day, Marlo is
loved very much indeed.

Thank you for reading.

Printed by Amazon Italia Logistica S.r.l.
Torrazza Piemonte (TO), Italy

40732994R00020